Wuthering Butts

A Ghost House Retelling of the Emily Brontë Classic

Ghost Writer
JASON STEELE

(Real author's name withheld to avoid spectral revenge.)

For all of the huge wild dogs Emily Brontë befriended.

"You said I killed you—haunt me then, coward! The murdered do haunt their murderers, probably. I know that ghosts wander around all willy nilly. Be with me always—take any gross form—donk me up! Only do not leave me in this gooey wet abyss, where I cannot find you!"

- Emily Brontë, Wuthering Heights

I'm an old man now, but back when I was a regular man I had quite a few spooky encounters. Get ready, because I'm going to tell you about one of the spookiest. This is the story of Wuthering Butts.

I had been standing on a big wet hill for too long, and
decided it was time to get away from all the bugs and
the morning dew. It was time to rent a manor house.

"It's a house!"

I checked the newspaper and a place called Thrushbutt Grange was available. I didn't know what a thrushbutt was, or a grange for that matter, but the advertisement said it said it was a house so I decided to take a chance.

My landlord was a grumpy ghost horse named Heathclop, who always had a look on his horse face that said, "Somebody put all my oats in the toilet."

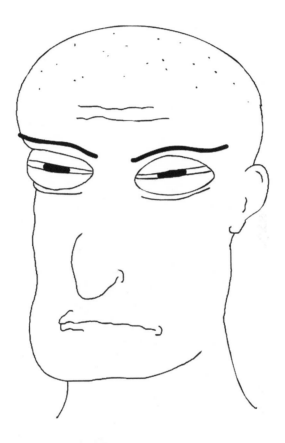

Every time he looked at me I thought, "Stop it. Stop looking at me with those wild eyes and wilder ways." He would stop a moment later but I don't think it was because of my thoughts.

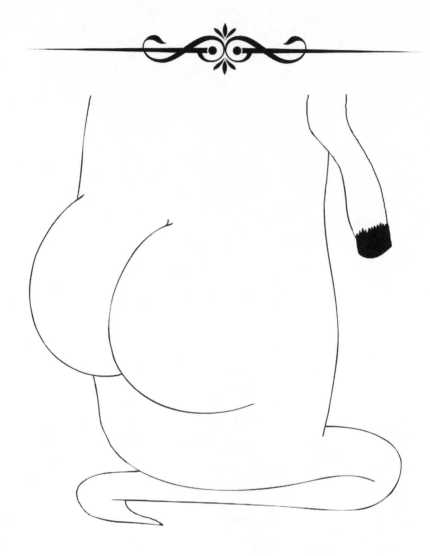

I assumed his ghost horse butt was going to be a bit rough and tumble but I was wrong. It was perfect. It was so perfect that I could not stop thinking about it even though it upset me so.

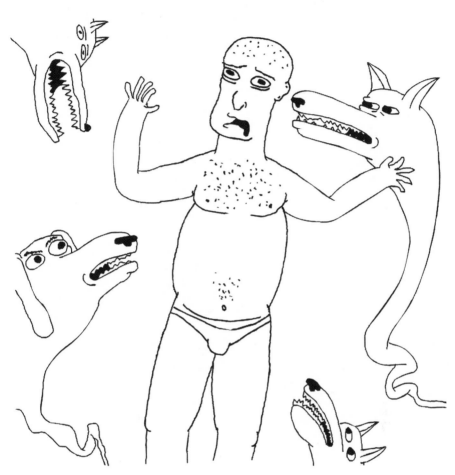

I tried saying hello to Heathclop one night at his house, a manor called Wuthering Butts, but the moment I set foot inside I was attacked by a dozen or so ghost dogs.

It sucked, and I ended up with ghost dog goo all over my entire body. Top to bottom.

Heathclop saw the dogs doing this, but he did nothing to stop it. He just stared at me with his scoundrel face, watching the dogs do their terrible work. Sad and ashamed about all the goo, I went back to my manor.

There was a creepy old ghost haunting Thrushbutt Grange who claimed to be Canadian singer-songwriter Nelly Furtado, and when she saw that I was covered in goo she laughed for pretty much the whole day. "Stop," I begged. "Your laugh is too hearty and exuberant."

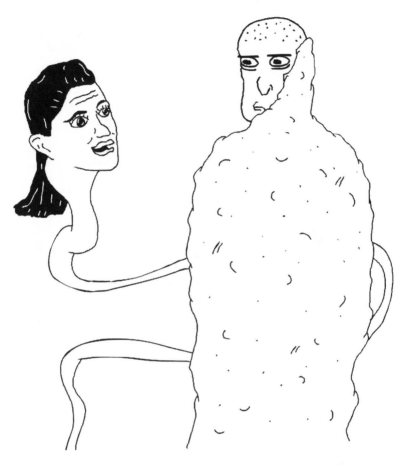

"Let me tell you the story of Heathclop, and Wuthering Butts," said the ghost who claimed to be Canadian singer-songwriter Nelly Furtado. I really didn't feel like hearing the story but apparently I had no choice, even in my own manor house.

Wuthering Butts

"It's also a house!"

Here is the story of Heathclop and Wuthering Butts, as told to me by that spooky storyteller Nelly Furtado. I have no idea if she was really the Canadian singer-songwriter famous for "I'm Like a Bird" and "Turn Off the Light," but she was definitely a ghost and also a home invader.

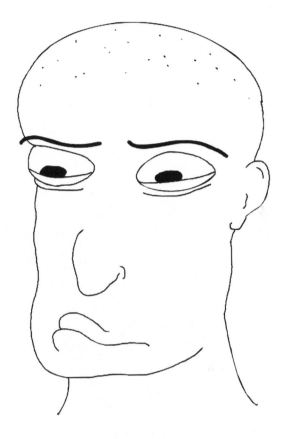

I realize you're now hearing a story within a story and that's a bit of a brain wiggler, but please don't get mad at me about it. I don't know what else to do.

Wuthering Butts used to be owned by a ghost named
Mr. Ears. I am glad I never met Mr. Ears because even
just thinking about a ghost who is mostly ears gives me
the willy woes.

Mr. Ears had two ghost kids, a boring baby boy named Handle and a cat girl named Cat Girl. They were both terrible, because that is the way of ghosts.

One day Mr. Ears decided two terrible ghost kids just wasn't enough, so he went into the cursed woods and stole a cursed ghost horse baby. "I'll name you Heathclop," he said to the child, "and you'll ruin my family for generations."

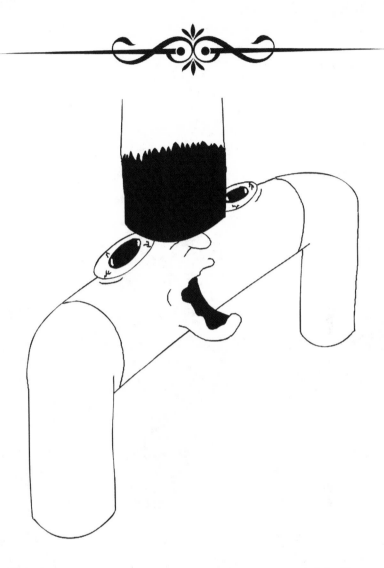

Handle hated Heathclop, which was reasonable because Heathclop was always putting his gross horse hooves all over Handle's soft sensitive face.

Cat Girl on the other hand immediately went all horse wild for Heathclop, because Heathclop would let her get on his back and then they would ride around the house like dangerous out of control animals.

Before I continue this spooky tale, I just remembered something important that happened right after I got attacked by ghost dogs at Wuthering Butts. I'm sorry for interrupting the story but it's really important.

I was too tired and sad about all the ghost dog goo to go home right away, so I sat down on one of Heathclop's gross old horse hay beds.

It was then that I beheld a most frightful sight…

It was a screaming Cat Girl, whose name I didn't know at the time, yelling about regrets and betrayal. I did not like it one bit. I was already feeling pretty down but that just ruined the night completely.

Heathclop heard the screams and came clomping over, but by the time he arrived Cat Girl was gone. "Did you see a cat girl?" he demanded of me. "You have to tell me if you saw a cat girl, it's the law."

A single tear fell down Heathclop's face. He told me that existence is a miasma of misery, and then loudly clomped away.

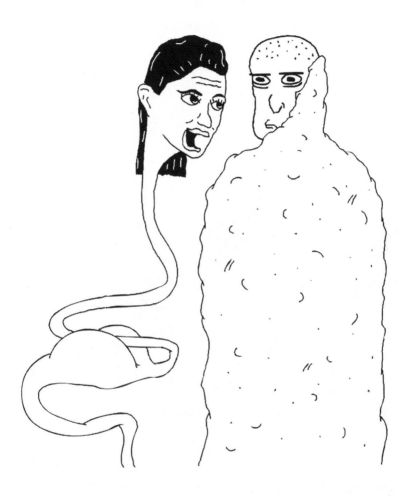

Alright, back to the story that the ghost who claimed to be Canadian singer-songwriter Nelly Furtado told me.

Heathclop and Cat Girl were inseparable. They had
fused together to become one big super ghost, and it
really upset just about everyone who saw it. It was too
much, even for other ghosts.

"We love playing on the moors!" Heathclop and Cat Girl would yell. I didn't know what moors were, but the ghost who claimed to be Canadian singer-songwriter Nelly Furtado told me they're basically just hills. Okay.

Mr. Ears had a wife, and she died. Which doesn't mean anything for ghosts because they just come right back, but his wife was a car so she went to the junk yard. Without a car or wife Mr. Ears became a huge grump and took all his grumps out on his boring son Handle.

"You're nothing like my other perfect beautiful son Heathclop," said Mr. Ears. "You don't play with Cat Girl all day on the moors. You just float about." Handle was sent away to Goo School to become a goo merchant, and Heathclop was kept at home where he was able to run around and eat oats all day.

Then Mr. Ears died too, and instead of coming back he decided to go haunt the junk yard. He had never written a last will and testament or even a first, so Handle ended up inheriting Wuthering Butts and Heathclop was left with nothing. Not even a single oat.

"You son of a gun," said Handle to Heathclop. "You put all your hooves all over my face every single day when we were growing up. I can still feel your hooves, on my face, my beautiful soft face. For that, I will have my revenge." Things were getting really intense.

Heathclop was forced to do degrading horse stuff in the fields all day, like jumping over fences and knocking down big stacks of hay. It was very embarrassing and it made Heathclop hate life and the world.

But mostly Heathclop hated Handle, with the sort of burning intensity common to horses. "I will have my own revenge," thought Heathclop. "And not just on Handle, but on his children and grandchildren too for some reason."

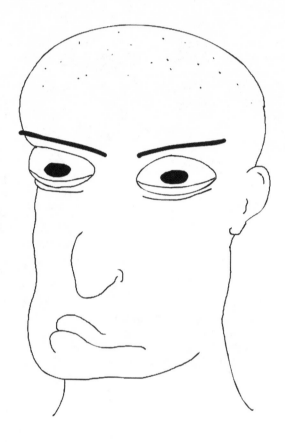

Hey, it's me again. I just wanted you to know that at this point in the story the ghost who claimed to be Canadian singer-songwriter Nelly Furtado started singing songs from her sixth studio album, "The Ride."

She sung through the whole dang album. Every song, even the slower ones. It wasn't bad, just very long. Then she continued the story and I'm pretty sure she skipped a bunch of stuff but whatever.

One day Cat Girl was attacked by a dozen ghost dogs, for pretty much no reason. Which is unacceptable. Someone should really do something about dogs.

During her recovery she fell in love with a poster of Edward from the Twilight movies. It was a pretty good poster where he was looking extra sultry, with his perfect chin sticking out and his dangerous eyes sticking in.

"I love both you and this sexy vampire poster," Cat Girl told Heathclop. "You both have your pluses and your minuses. I cannot choose between you. You are both perfect and beautiful."

But then Cat Girl decided she actually super could choose, and chose the poster of Edward from Twilight, and they were married immediately.

Thrushbutt Grange

"It's still a house!"

They lived together in the Edward poster's manor,
Thrushbutt Grange, which he had purchased using all
his Hollywood gold.

Heathclop could not understand why Cat Girl had married a sexy vampire poster. "She should have married someone who is technically her brother, like me," he thought to himself.

He was so depressed that he let the wind just sort of carry him away. It could carry him all the way to the garbage dump for all he cared.

Cat Girl's heart ached when she learned that Heathclop was gone, because she loved him and his out of control horse bod. She didn't regret her marriage but she did really want that bod.

Every night she screamed his name out the window, hoping he would hear her and come back. It was a real nuisance to everyone who lived nearby, let me tell you.

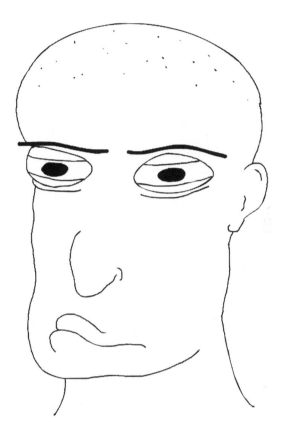

Hello again reader. I need you to know that at this point the ghost who claimed to be Canadian singer-songwriter Nelly Furtado once again began singing her entire sixth studio album, "The Ride."

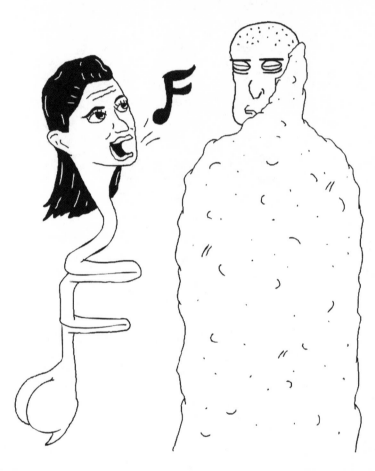

I didn't want to be rude so I just stood there listening to
the entire thing. It grew on me a little, hearing it that
second time. But only a little baby bit. I was glad when
she finished and continued the story.

Three years later Heathclop returned, with a bunch of gold and jewels and emeralds. Everyone assumed he had probably robbed a Duke or something but no one looked into it, on account of how scary and intense his horse face was.

The first thing Heathclop did when he got back was give a bunch of gold to Handle. But for evil reasons, instead of good reasons. Heathclop knew that Handle was really bad with gold and would accidentally drop it all on his own face or something.

Which is more or less what happened. Handle took all the gold, ate it, died, and then floated away forever.

Heathclop clasped his big hooves together in glee, pleased that his revenge was off to such a promising start. "Wuthering Butts," which had previously been owned by Handle, was now his.

The next step in his revenge plan was to get married.
On the darkest and stormiest night possible Heathclop
married a poster of Bella from Twilight, thinking that it
would drive Cat Girl wild with jealousy.

Cat Girl wasn't jealous at all and honestly would have preferred if all four of them could be married together like some sort of super family. Alas, such a union was not to be. Only tragedy was to be.

Cat Girl gave birth to a spooky baby named Cat Girl 2. Cat Girl 2 looked almost exactly like her mother, except she had a cool "2" on her forehead.

Then Cat Girl died and floated away, leaving Cat Girl 2 to be raised by the poster of Edward from Twilight, and Canadian singer-songwriter Nelly Furtado who was also there for some reason.

"No! You can't die and float away!" yelled Heathclop to Cat Girl as she drifted into the sky. "I just got back and my revenge isn't done yet!"

Cat Girl just gave one of her classic shrugs and continued on her way.

Using all his most powerful horse magic, Heathclop
constructed a forcefield that prevented Cat Girl from
ever escaping. I didn't even know horses had magic.

The poster of Bella from Twilight, frightened by
Heathclop's dark ways, ripped herself off the wall, folded
up into an airplane, and flew to sunny Miami, Florida.

With his wife gone and Cat Girl's twice dead ghost never visiting, Heathclop spent the next thirteen years hooting and hollering around Wuthering Butts, wondering why life was so unfair to horses.

Eventually Heathclop got a letter from the Bella poster letting him know that she had died. She also sent him a terrible weak son, Lint, named after lint.

Lint really was an unbelievably weak son. His arms were like noodle arms, and his whole body was like three noodles wide, maximum.

A week after Lint arrived Cat Girl 2 found his weak noodle body collapsed on the moors, near death.

"I cannot believe how sickly your boy bod is," said Cat Girl 2 to poor Lint, who could barely even keep his eyes open. "Nonetheless, I immediately love you because I've never met anyone who isn't either my dad or Canadian singer-songwriter Nelly Furtado."

"Please," said Lint, his body tendrils wilting in her arms. "Take care of me like you would a diseased baby. Keep me alive by feeding me your life essence. I need as much essence as I can get, I'm such a frail terrible boy."

Before she could answer, Heathclop jumped out of some bushes wearing a priest robe and holding a Bible. "You're married now!" he yelled, and then he ate the Bible.

"What? Married?" said Cat Girl 2. But she knew in her heart it was true—she was now legally married to the terrible dying boy.

Actually, he wasn't dying—he was already dead, and his
wisp of a body had disintegrated into actual lint.

"I own your manor now," said Heathclop, his dark shark eyes watching bits of his dead son float away. "My revenge is complete."

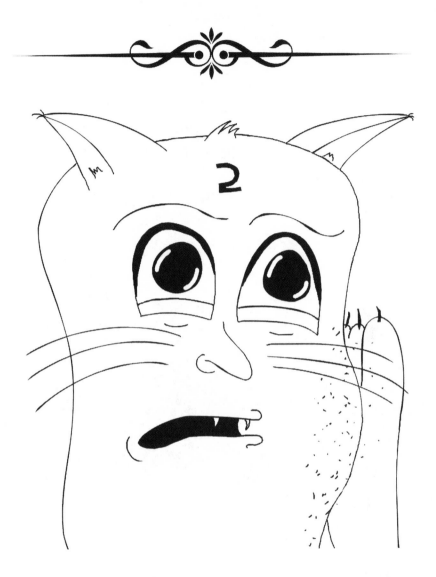

"Uhh, my dad owns Thrushbutt Grange," said Cat Girl 2, wiping Lint's lint off her face. "All of it, even the dirt."

"Uh, actually your dad is dead too," said Heathclop. "And the law says if your dad dies and you marry my dead son I own your house."

Just a few moments prior the poster of Edward had fallen into a big dog's mouth, which did indeed mean Heathclop had legal ownership of Thrushbutt Grange.

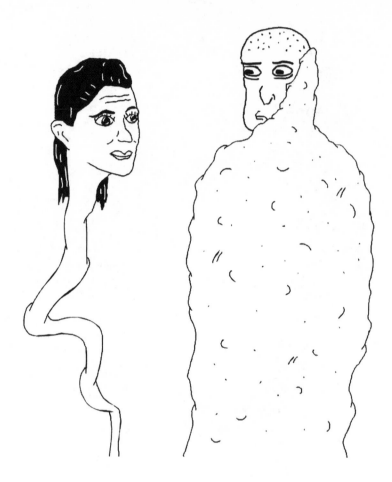

After telling me about the big dog mouth, the ghost
who claimed to be Canadian singer-songwriter Nelly
Furtado became very silent and still.

"Then what?" I asked, hoping she wouldn't start a third round of singing her third studio album, "The Ride."

She did start a third round of singing "The Ride." I listened to the whole thing again but I wasn't happy about it. Three times in one day was just too much.

When the final song was over, she told me that the big dog mouth stuff had happened less than a week ago, and so the story was complete.

"I don't want to stay here anymore, in this grange," I said. Then I hobbled right out the front door, not even stopping to take the free umbrella I had received as part of my rental agreement.

I came back for that umbrella a couple hours later and learned that Heathclop had died while I was gone.

"He ran around the moors, screaming and shouting that Cat Girl had been a bad sister and girlfriend, then he fell over dead," said the ghost who claimed to be Canadian singer-songwriter Nelly Furtado.

"Also Cat Girl 2 got married to Bun Bun." I didn't know who that was and didn't care enough to ask.

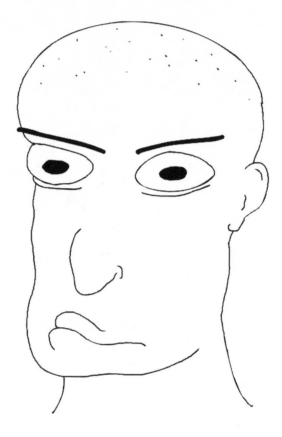

The moral of the story is that horses are scary and dangerous and will do just about anything for oats.

Also, everything involving ghosts is the worst.

The End.

90982784R00054

Made in the USA
San Bernardino, CA
23 October 2018